Taiko on a Windy Night

BY **Sally Derby**

ILLUSTRATED BY **Kate Kiesler**

HENRY HOLT AND COMPANY

NEW YORK

Henry Holt and Company, LLC
Publishers since 1866
115 West 18th Street, New York, New York 10011

Henry Holt is a registered trademark of Henry Holt and Company, LLC
Text copyright © 2001 by Sally Derby
Illustrations copyright © 2001 by Kate Kiesler
All rights reserved.
Published in Canada by Fitzhenry & Whiteside Ltd.,
195 Allstate Parkway, Markham, Ontario L3R 4T8.

Library of Congress Cataloging-in-Publication Data
Derby, Sally.
Taiko on a windy night / by Sally Derby; illustrated by Kate Kiesler
Summary: A cat enjoys the sights, sounds, and smells of a nighttime stroll.
[1. Cats—Fiction. 2. Night—Fiction.] I. Kiesler, Kate, ill. II. Title.
PZ7.D44174 Tai 2001   [E]—dc21   99-47349
ISBN 0-8050-6401-X / First Edition—2001 / Designed by Donna Mark
Printed in the United States of America on acid-free paper. ∞
1 3 5 7 9 10 8 6 4 2

The artist used pastels on pastel paper to create
the illustrations for this book.

For Sarah, who brings us love and kittens

—S. D.

For Carol and Charlie

—K. K.

One evening, very late, the cat meowed at the back door. "Come back soon," the girl called as he scampered off.

The wind that night
was wild and chill.
It tossed down dry leaves
for the cat to pounce on.

The moon that night
was full and round.
It turned the grass to silver.
The cat's yellow eyes
shone back up at the moon.

The cat walked the backyard fence like a proud black shadow.
He stretched—front legs out, back legs straight,
tail curled high.

The neighbor's beagle lifted her head and sniffed,
then strolled over to the fence.

The cat jumped down and greeted her,
rubbing his velvety head
against the beagle's chin.
The wind picked up a garbage-can lid
and banged it down the driveway.
Startled, the cat leapt
onto the crab-apple trunk,
scrambled up to the branches.

The wind died down. The beagle
sauntered back to her doghouse
and curled herself up inside.

All was quiet.

The cat backed down the tree,
up to the fence again and over.
He bounded across the grass,
stopped to groom himself in the moonlight.

A field mouse darted across his path
and he streaked after it,
ducking under bushes,
losing it in the weeds.

The wind stirred again,
floated exciting smells.
The cat drew a long breath—
his ears twitched,
back, then forward.
Something new, something different!
He began to hurry.
Down the sidewalk he padded—
stopped,
sprinted on.
Faster and farther,
faster and farther,
past houses with yellow windows.

The wind cried adventure,
the moon shone mystery.

Tree branches waved, cast dancing shadows.
The cat stopped and watched.
He watched for a long, quiet time.

Back at the house,
the girl came out on the porch.
"Taiko," she called.
"Here, kitty, here, kitty."

The cat didn't turn around.
Too soon,
too soon.

At the corner, an old raccoon
lumbered across the street.
The cat froze and watched.
The raccoon ducked into a
storm sewer as a car drove past.

The wind blew again.
A scrap of crumpled paper
came scritch-scratching
along the sidewalk.
The cat jumped to one side,
crouched low, watched,
then pounced.
Paper ball in his mouth,
he rolled in the grass,
pawed it into the air,
lost it, rolled over,
pounced again.

Nearby, a car door slammed.
The cat tensed, stared at the sudden lights,
turned around, headed back up the street.
Slow-moving now, with dignified gait,
he paused here and there to look around,
to search the air for new smells.

Suddenly, through the darkness
a bicycle whizzed down the sidewalk.
With a yowl, the cat jumped aside,
dived into the bushes.
Behind the bike loped a dog,
a dog he didn't know.
It nosed into the bushes
where he was hiding.
The cat crouched lower and hissed.
The dog paused uncertainly until
the boy on the bike called,
"Here, boy!"
With one short growl, the dog turned
and ran after the disappearing bike.

Quiet came back to the street.
The cat stayed hidden,
his heart pounding.
The door opened, and
the girl came out on the porch.
"Taiko? Here, Taiko!
Here, kitty, here, kitty.
Where are you?"

The girl went down the steps,
down the walk,
out of the porch light
into the moonlight.
"Taiko?" she called. "Taiko?"

Under the bushes the cat waited.
He purred, and he washed
while he waited.
The girl walked on, and
the wind lifted her hair.
She held her arms and shivered.
"Taiko? Where *are* you, Taiko?"

With a *mrrow* of welcome
from deep in his throat,
out of the bushes he came,
rubbing against the girl's legs.
Bending, she scooped him up
and carried him home in her arms.

Outside, the wind was wild and chill,
the moon was shining mystery.
But Taiko, curled up on the girl's bed,
purred himself to sleep.

WITHDRAWN